A Picture Story Book

Voltaire
The Dog and the Horse

translated by Anthea Bell

moonlight publishing

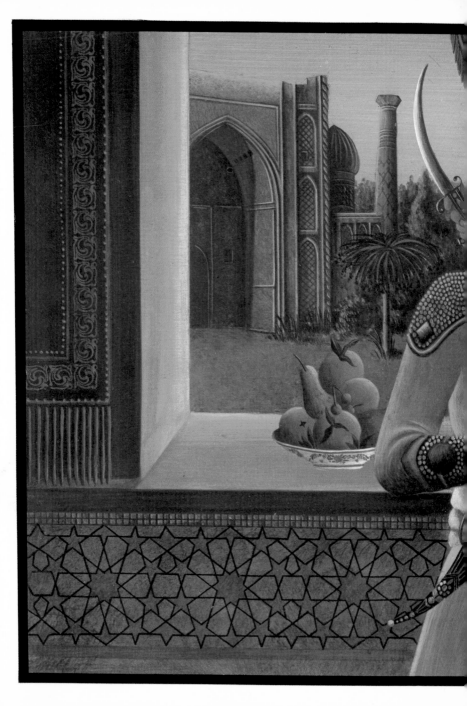

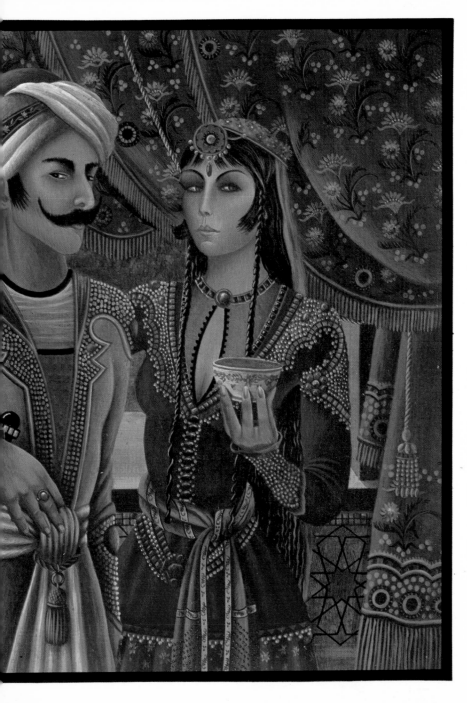

In the time of King Moabdar there was a young man called Zadig living in Babylon. Although he was rich and youthful, he was well in control of his passions. He married a lady called Azora, but he soon found out that, as it is written in the Book of Zend, the first month of marriage is the honeymoon or Moon of Honey, and the second is the Moon of Bitter Wormwood. A little later he had to part from Azora, who had become very difficult to live with, and he looked for his happiness in the study of Nature. "No one", said he, "is happier than a philosopher reading the great book which God has placed before our eyes. The truths he discovers there are his own; he is nourishing and educating his mind; his way of life is peaceful, and he has nothing to fear from men."

With such ideas as these, he withdrew to a country house on the banks of the river Euphrates. He did not spend his time there working out how many inches of water ran under a bridge in the course of a second, or if rainfall was heavier in the Month of the Mouse or the Month of the Sheep. He did not devise plans for making silk out of spiders' webs, or china out of broken bottles; instead, he put his mind to the study of plants and animals and their natures, and he soon gathered knowledge which showed him a thousand differences where other people would see none at all.

One day, while he was walking near a little wood, he saw one of the Queen's eunuchs hurrying towards him, followed by several other officers of her household, who seemed to be in a state of great anxiety, running about like people frantically searching for something very precious which has been lost. "Young man," asked the head eunuch, "have you seen the Queen's dog?" "It is not a dog, but a bitch," replied Zadig, modestly. "You are right," said the head eunuch. "She is a very small spaniel," added Zadig. "She has just had puppies, she is lame in her left fore-paw, and she has very long ears." "Oh, so you have seen her?" said the head eunuch, breathlessly. "No," replied Zadig. "I have never seen her, and until now I did not even know that the Queen had a dog."

At exactly the same time, by one of those odd coincidences that do often happen, the finest horse in the King's stable had escaped from a groom out on the plains of Babylon. The chief huntsman and all the other officers of the King's household were looking for it as anxiously as the head eunuch was looking for the dog. The chief huntsman spoke to Zadig, asking if he had seen the King's horse pass that way. "Ah," said Zadig, "that is the horse which gallops better than any other, he is five feet tall, he has very small hooves, his tail is three and a half feet long, the bosses of his bit are made of twenty-three carat gold, and he is shod with shoes of the finest silver." "Which way did he go? Where is he?" asked the chief huntsman. "I have not set eyes on him at all", replied Zadig. "In fact, I never heard of him before."

The chief huntsman and the head eunuch felt sure that Zadig had stolen the King's horse and the Queen's dog, so they had him brought before the Grand Treasurer's court, which condemned him to be whipped and then exiled to Siberia for life. But no sooner had sentence been passed than the dog and the horse were found. The judges were in the unfortunate position of having to repeal the sentence, but they condemned Zadig to pay four hundred ounces of gold for having said he had not seen something when all the time he had seen it. Zadig had to pay this fine before he was allowed to plead his cause to the Grand Treasurer's court. He spoke to them in these words:

"Bright stars of justice, deep mines of knowledge, mirrors of truth – you who are weighty as lead, hard as iron, who sparkle like the diamond and have a great deal in common with gold! Since I am allowed to speak before this noble assembly, I swear to you by Ormuzd that I have never seen the Queen's distinguished dog nor the sacred horse of the King of Kings in all my life.

"This is what happened to me. I was walking towards the little wood where I later met the honourable eunuch and the noble chief huntsman. I saw the prints of an animal's paws on the sand, and I could easily tell that they belonged to a small dog. The slight traces of long furrows on the sand where it was higher between the paw-prints told me that the tracks had been left by a bitch with dangling teats, and so I knew she had had puppies not many days before. Other tracks, not quite parallel, which seemed to have been made by something constantly grazing the surface of the sand beside the dog's forepaws, showed that she had very long ears. And, as I noticed that one paw always left a fainter print on the sand than the other three, I realized that, if I may venture to say so, our great Queen's dog was slightly lame.

"As for the horse belonging to the King of Kings, you must know that, as I was walking along the woodland paths, I saw the marks of a horse's hooves. They were all the same distance apart. 'There', said I to myself, 'went a horse which gallops perfectly.'

"Three and a half feet from the middle of a path which was only seven feet wide a little dust had been brushed off the trees to right and to left of the path. 'That horse', said I to myself, 'has a tail three and a half feet long, and the sweeping of his tail to right and left brushed off the dust.' Under the trees, which formed an archway five feet high, I saw some leaves which had recently fallen off their branches, and I knew that the horse had touched them, and thus that he was five feet tall. As for his bit, it must be made of twenty-three carat gold, because he had rubbed its bosses against a stone which I recognized as a touchstone for testing gold, and indeed I tried it out. Finally, the marks left by his hooves on some stones of a different kind told me that he was shod with silver of the finest quality."

All the judges admired Zadig's profound and clever observations. News of them came to the King and Queen. In the royal antechambers, the state room and the council chamber, no one could talk about anything but Zadig, and, although some of the mages said they thought he should be burnt as a sorceror, the King gave orders for the four hundred ounces of gold which he had been condemned to pay as a fine to be given back to him.

The clerk of the court, the ushers and the treasury officials visited him in great state to return him his four hundred ounces of gold, keeping back only three hundred and ninety-eight ounces for the costs of the case while their servants asked for tips.

Zadig saw how dangerous too much knowledge can sometimes be, and he vowed to himself that next time he would not say a word about anything he had seen.

Next time soon came. A prisoner of state escaped; he passed the windows of Zadig's house. Zadig was questioned, and said nothing, but it was proved that he had been looking out of the window. He was fined five hundred ounces of gold for this crime, and he thanked the judges for their mercy, according to the custom of Babylon. "Good God," said he to himself, "how unfortunate it is to go walking in a wood where the Queen's dog and the King's horse have passed by! How dangerous it is to look out of the window! And how difficult it is to be happy in this life."